POOR CARL

POOR CARL

Nancy Carlson

PUFFIN BOOKS

PUFFIN BOOKS
Published by the Penguin Group
Viking Penguin, a division of Penguin Books USA Inc.,
375 Hudson Street, New York, New York 10014, U.S.A.
Penguin Books Ltd, 27 Wrights Lane, London W8 5TZ, England
Penguin Books Australia Ltd, Ringwood, Victoria, Australia
Penguin Books Canada Ltd, 2801 John Street, Markham, Ontario, Canada L3R 1B4
Penguin Books (N.Z.) Ltd, 182–190 Wairau Road, Auckland 10, New Zealand

Penguin Books Ltd, Registered Offices: Harmondsworth, Middlesex, England

First published in the United States of America by Viking Penguin Inc., 1989
Published in Picture Puffins, 1991
1 3 5 7 9 10 8 6 4 2
Copyright © Nancy Carlson, 1989
All rights reserved

LIBRARY OF CONGRESS CATALOGING IN PUBLICATION DATA
Carlson, Nancy L.
Poor Carl / by Nancy Carlson.   p.   cm. — (Picture puffins)
Summary: Carl's big brother doesn't think it would be easy to be a
baby, but he also realizes Carl is lucky to have someone to play
with and protect him.
ISBN 0-14-050773-6
[1. Brothers—Fiction.   2. Babies—Fiction.   3. Dogs—Fiction.]
I. Title.
PZ7.C21665Po   1991   [E]—dc20   90-41999

Printed in Hong Kong
Set in Century Schoolbook

I'm glad I'm not a baby like my new brother, Carl.

Poor Carl can't get out of bed in the morning like me.

He has to cry until someone
comes to get him.

Then he needs his pants
changed and it stinks.

Poor Carl can't dress himself, like I do!

For breakfast I sit in a big chair and eat pancakes with syrup.
Poor Carl has to eat yucky rice cereal and strained prunes.

After breakfast I get to play outside with my friends.

Poor Carl can only sit and watch.

When it's Carl's nap time,

Mom and I make cookies
and she lets me lick the bowl.

After his nap poor Carl just has a bottle and I get a warm cookie.

But sometimes I wish I were Carl.

Everyone thinks he's so cute.

And whenever someone comes to see him they bring him
a big present and they don't pay any attention to me.

At dinner Carl is lucky. He doesn't have to eat Brussels sprouts

or clear the table.

Sometimes Carl can be really fun
even though he's just a baby.

We take our baths together and I help him wash.

Carl likes to play with me best.

He always smiles at me when we play peek-a-boo.

But then Carl has to go to bed early.
Even before it's dark.

I get to stay up late and Dad reads me stories.

I'm real quiet when I go to bed.

But if Carl wakes up scared
I'm there to protect him.

I guess Carl's really lucky after all,
because I'm his big brother.